One Small Gift

One Small Gift

Beverley Labrum

Illustrated
by John Watson

Second Edition
Copyright © 1997 by Beverley Labrum
All rights reserved. Beverley Labrum Books.

ISBN 0-9659639-1-8

Printed in the U.S.A.

Written For:

McKenzie, Justin, Sydney, and Kylee.

Acknowledgements:

Special thanks to Johnnie, who saw with his heart and brought the story into visualization, to Margaret Labrum, Barbara Watson, and Kay Johnson for editing, to Val Shuey for encouragement, and to Tim Griffith for layout and pre-publication work.

Part One

The Parting

The teacher turned, startled to see a youngster at the door. It was not yet even eight o'clock on that sunny spring morning. The sun, reaching through the blinds, seemed to cast a golden glow about the towheaded lad of seven.

"Why, good morning, Chris. My, but you're early today," she greeted him. "You can play out on the playground until the bell rings," she said as she glanced at the clock, wondering how she was to get everything ready in time on this last day of school with forms to fill out, records to hand in, and all the tasks to be completed on her list.

"Can't play yet," he said in a low voice. "I want to talk to you first. It's important!"

The teacher turned around at the tone of the boy's voice and saw that this was a grave moment for the awkward, over-sized first grader who had moved into her class late in the year. His toe, if it could have, would surely have worn a hole in the carpet as he twisted it about.

"Yes, well, come in and let's sit down at the reading table." She noticed then the teddy bear he held by one paw as he drew it out from behind him.

"It's my bear," he said, suddenly thrusting it forward. "I've brought him to you."

"Goodness! Teddy Bear Week is over, Chris. Did you bring him here to spend the last day of school with you?"

"No, I'm bringing him to you," he said determinedly.

"Chris, you don't just give your teddy bear away. Teddies are..." She didn't finish as she saw the tears he was bravely blinking back.

"See, we have to move. My mom says I have to give everything away, and what's left has to go to the Salvation Army. I'll get new toys where we're going. Anyways, she says I'm too old to keep Bear now. I'm already seven."

"Oh, I see," understanding dawning. "So you're trying to find a very safe place for your bear, where he'll be taken care of. You know I love bears," the teacher offered.

"Yeah," he said, shaking his head up and down rapidly, "I figured you'd watch out for him. Since you know the Teddy Bear King and all, well, maybe you'd let him go to the bear picnics each year like he did last week. He had fun." His voice started to crack as he rubbed his finger back and forth across Bear's small badge that he had won at the Teddy Bear Picnic the previous week. It said "Most Loved."

"Of course, I'd love to have him here! I can tell he's a very special bear, one who has lots of love to give. I think maybe you've taught him a lot about love, Chris."

"Yeah, I just want him to be happy and have a home, so's I know where he is."

"Does he have a name?" asked Miss Lilly, taking the furry, oatmeal-colored bear gently from Chris to have a better look at him.

"I just call him Bear," Chris said.

"I'll just keep Bear here for you. I'll be around here yet for a good many years. He can stay right here in school with me and help out with these little first-graders. But he'll always be here for you. He'll wait till someday when you're grown up and you come back for him. You'll have a place of your own then, and he'll be glad to go with you. How's that?"

The face of the young lad – boy outside man inside – lit right up! "Yup! That's kinda what I was thinking. I told him all about it in bed last night, and he seemed to think it was okay. Well, guess I'll go outside now."

Turning back, he blurted out "THANKS." Then he ran outside.

It was the young teacher, this time, who fought to blink back the tears as she hugged the tattered and worn bear close to her. This morning she had received a "miracle gift" which can only be given by a child; a gift too precious to be wrapped in a box with all the fancy tissue paper and

15

bows, given from the heart. The gift was trust, its other name being LOVE.

No one could have told Miss Lilly what being a teacher would really be about. Oh yes, there was the teaching of math, reading, writing, spelling, science and all the other subjects. But no one told her that within the walls of her classroom, she would perhaps be the greatest learner of all. She would learn about life from the heroines and heroes hidden from the world. She would learn from these little ones who live life so openly, so honestly, doing the best they can with the lives they have been given.

Long after the children had departed, the teacher sat alone in the once-bustling classroom, pondering the mixture of feelings that always beset her after completing a year of teaching. Exhaustion was beginning to settle in, accompanied by a sense of freedom and anticipation of renewal during the summer months ahead. Yet, there was still a tugging at the heartstrings as she thought of the twenty-four little ones who left her room for the last time this day. The "letting go" was always the hardest and she allowed herself a few tears as she glanced down at Bear, who looked back at her with his black button eyes, smudged nose, and steady smile. A feeling of peace and calm replaced the aching emptiness.

"Well, Bear, welcome to my workshop! It will be good to have a partner – and such an all-wise knowing one at that," she said as she gave him a pat. "We'll have the summer to really get acquainted." Together, they turned out the lights, locked the door, and left the stillness of an empty room behind them.

Part Two

The Beginning

The furry oatmeal-colored bear sat on the shelf of the toy shop gazing out from his bright black button eyes. His black yarn nose twitched ever so slightly as the door of the toy shop opened. He'd heard about what wonderful possibilities earth life could offer as he left the Teddy Kingdom for his life mission. His smile stayed steady and gave not a hint of the surprise he felt when the stately, white-haired gentleman gave him an appraising look. It was not at all the girl or boy he had hoped might choose him.

"Yes, yes, I think you'll do the job, my friend," he said with certainty, as he picked him from the shelf and took him over to the counter where he handed the clerk some crisp new bills.

"Have you a box for packing?" he asked. "This bear has a long journey to make. He's going to a hospital where he'll be joining my grandson who is to have surgery. You see, I can't be there myself, so this bear is going in my place. He's going to assure Chris that everything will be fine. He just might help him to feel a little better."

"Yes sir, I can fix that right up for you. It will take just a few minutes," the clerk said as she went to get the box and packing material.

So that was all the knowledge Bear had of what was about to happen to him. Before he knew it, he was put into a box and darkness closed around him. It was rather frightening, feeling oneself being propelled about without being able to see! This seemed to go on endlessly until at last one day, he heard paper being torn from the box. The lid came off and he was engulfed by light, as well as by a blue-eyed, towheaded boy of about four who, upon seeing him, clutched him tightly to himself and said, "Bear!"

"Yes, and listen to this note from your grandfather," said his mother.

Dear Chris,

"I'm sorry that I can't get away at this time to come and be with you, so I'm sending a special friend of mine. He will be with you every minute at the hospital and will be your friend from

now on. He will help you to be brave and to know that everything will be fine. You can tell him anything. He'll always listen and be there for you."

Love, Grandpa

Thus Bear's earth life began in a hospital with a small tyke who bravely went into surgery with Bear tucked under his arm. And sure enough, when he awoke hours later, Bear was there on his pillow waiting for him. In fact, Bear did a lot of waiting during those next few years. But that, being part of a teddy bear's life, was fine because it served such an important purpose.

On occasion, Bear was taken outside, to the park, on family outings, even a vacation here and there. He rode on trains and an airplane once, and in many cars. But his favorite place of all was in the boy's room where he heard so many wonderful stories and secrets, and shared much laughter. Sometimes Chris played games with him. When Chris learned to read, he read to Bear. Sometimes he heard the worries and tearful tales from Chris, and he always did his best to comfort him. Through the years he grew to love this boy with an immeasurable love. His whole world was centered around him. He knew his greatest hopes and his greatest fears. The most difficult moment to console the boy came late one night when Bear himself was almost inconsolable. That was the night when Chris once more confided in him a great and awful secret. His parents, it seemed, were going their own ways, and he was to go with his mother to a new place where there would be a "new dad". He would have to leave all his things – toys too, because there wasn't room. He'd have to get new ones. "You're too old to carry along a bear now," his mother had declared.

That was the night the boy's racking sobs nearly broke the bear's heart. The tears fell into his soft fur and were absorbed by Bear as best he could. During those tender hours, boy and bear shared a sweet comradeship. Bear listened to Chris as he tried to comfort them both. He said that he'd find a very special place where Bear would be safe. He wasn't going to be left or given to just any old person. Bear longed with all his teddy heart to speak to the boy – but he could only stay near and cuddle closer, if possible. When the moon finally peeped through the blinds, it shined softly on the faces of both as they took comfort in the boy's idea.

The next morning found them on their way to school far earlier than usual. All the way, Chris held Bear close and reminded him that they'd have to be very brave, and that one day, they'd find each other again. "Besides, Bear, Grandpa said you'd teach me to be brave and you have. He said we'd always be friends, and we will. And when we're missing each other and the missing gets too hard, then we can just close our eyes and see each other. We can remember all our special times and we can pretend that we're there together." Bear was quite convinced by the time he and Chris reached the school that things would turn out as the boy had told him. And so Bear had been left in the hands of Chris's teacher.

Bear liked Miss Lilly very much. He'd had such fun the previous week at all the Teddy Bear events when all the kids brought their bears to school. Then there was the Teddy Picnic at midnight, when the Teddy King came in person to visit his subjects to see that they were well-taken care of. Ah yes, if he could stay with this teacher, who was a friend of the Teddy Bear King, he knew he would be all right. But letting the boy go – that was the hard part. What would become of him? Who would care…

Part Three

The Working Together

Miss Lilly took Bear home for the summer. She fixed his black yarn nose, which had almost been rubbed off with so much loving. She polished his black button eyes till they shone like new. She put patches on his paws, which were worn from helping a young boy so much, and she tied a beautiful new plaid bow around his neck. "There now, Bear, you're all ready to go back to school next fall. You look like new — almost." She sighed, "Ah, but your eyes seem to hold all the wisdom of many years."

That fall Bear went back to school with Miss Lilly. He was introduced to the children on the first day of school. At first, his task seemed almost insurmountable — so many children to love, to listen to, and to help. He made up his mind to do his best. Every year thereafter, the procedure was the same. Bear and Miss Lilly shared another school year with another group of students. Every year, they spent the summer together. Bear always had his yarn nose fixed, his button eyes polished, new patches put on his paws and a brand new ribbon tied about his neck. He felt loved

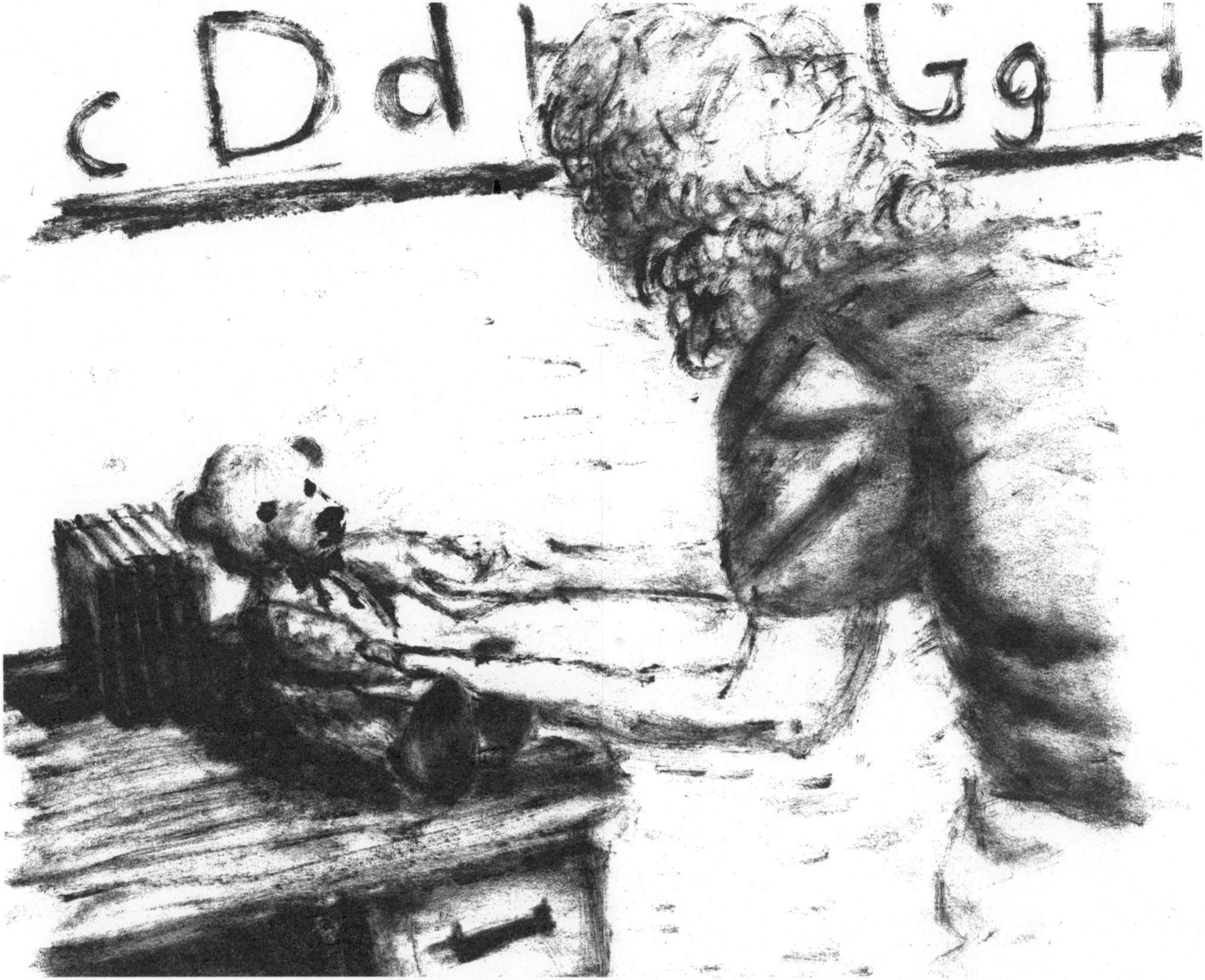
cDd
GgH

and needed, and he was content. Bear often liked to think, in his quiet time, about many great and tender moments that he had shared with children during those years.

There was the time when little Jeanette had burst into the room during the lunch hour and, through her tears, told Miss Lilly that she had lost her tooth on the playground and that now the Tooth Fairy wouldn't come. Miss Lilly told her to wash her face and hands and then talk to Bear. As the child did this, Miss Lilly wrote a love note from the Tooth Fairy and placed it and two quarters in Bear's paw. So together, she and Bear brought a smile to one small face.

John, the boy who stuttered so badly, had held Bear, and he'd read the whole page aloud in reading group with smoothness and great satisfaction at his success. Bear helped him through several such situations until at last, most of the stuttering had disappeared.

One stormy afternoon, the power in that section of town was out for an hour, plunging the inner windowless rooms of the school into complete darkness. The emergency generator had also failed. Children were frightened, but Bear and Miss Lilly soon had them listening to stories and pretending until they were calm and secure. Bear made his way from one child to another and his touch seemed to comfort them. They were almost disappointed when the lights came on!

The little Russian girl, Anna, entered the classroom not knowing a word of English. But Bear soon had her feeling right at home and even learning some English words quite quickly.

The orphan boy, Jim, had no bear to carry in the Teddy Bear Parade and Bear was proud to march with him.

Nathan had broken his arm and Bear had waited with him in the nurse's office until his mother arrived.

Still though, he sighed every now and then as a wistful longing surfaced, a yearning for his first special boy.

As the years passed, Bear observed his teacher changing and he had a growing concern. Miss Lilly no longer walked as jauntily or as quickly. Her once dark hair began to have a well-earned silver streak here and there. She wore glasses which Bear was sure were getting a little thicker each year. It seemed to take her longer to do things. Oh, how he longed to be able to help her! He had been a great listener though. He found that she confided in him almost as much as Chris once had. How he wished he could have spoken to her, and yet, she'd repeat aloud what she thought he would say. Bear was always amazed and pleased to see that it was just what he would have said, if he could have!

Yes, Bear and Miss Lilly were quite content with the boy's solution. It had worked out very well for them both. But in the hearts of both, there was always the tiny hope – that one day, one day …

The days passed into weeks and weeks into months and months into years, until they had both stopped counting. On they went together, teaching and shaping young minds, and especially touching young hearts, each in his or her own way becoming a part of the future.

Part Four

From Now On

The afternoon sun had just worked its way down to Miss Lilly's window. It reached through the blinds and flooded the room with lazy warmth. Miss Lilly sat at her desk engaged in the never-ending task of correcting papers. Bear sat as he always did in the reading loft and thought about the happenings of the day. He reveled in little memories of this child or that child and still, every now and then, he thought back to his beginning with the stately, white-haired gentleman who had purchased him and sent him on a very important mission. That mission had taught Bear about love, about a boy, and perhaps that beginning gave him his great love and understanding for the children who crossed his path each year.

The minutes ticked away in an easy silence. So intent on her work and so intent on his memories, neither noticed the tall man who stood just outside the door. He stood quietly, his hat in his hand, and gazed at the teacher.

Feeling that someone was needing her attention, she looked up. "May

I help you?" she asked, a slow smile creeping across her face.

" I was a student here once long ago. I wondered if you'd mind if I just looked around for a moment," he smiled and gestured toward the room, a merry twinkle hidden in his eyes just out of sight of Miss Lilly.

"Well, of course, come right in," she said as she began to put away her things for the day.

Bear felt more alert than he had for a long time. His heart began to beat just a bit faster and his nose twitched ever so slightly. He didn't have to turn his head at all to see who was at the door. He thought he couldn't hold still a minute longer!

Miss Lilly had looked up now and watched as the tall man made his way around the room. There was something – something familiar about this man! Her heart quickened its pace just a little as she puzzled for a moment. She saw him pause in front of the reading loft. Was it just her imagination that the man began to stand a little taller? Was it indeed a

deep sigh of contentment that came from him?

Then Miss Lilly knew. She walked over to the reading loft just as Chris reached out one strong arm to pick up his old and tattered and well-loved Bear.

Their eyes locked in recognition and understanding. The eyes of the tall young man and the old teacher glistened with happy tears; and Bear, if he could have, would gladly have shed a few himself! His button eyes glowed with complete love at the two of them, his most-beloved earth folk.

"Somehow I knew you'd always come back one day," Miss Lilly said as she led Chris and Bear over to the reading table where they sat down with Bear between them. "However, I was beginning to worry just a little because, you see, at the end of this year I'm going to retire. Thirty-six years of teaching seemed to go by just like a dream. My sister and I are going to share a home on the coast. We'll fill our days with walks on the beach and doing all those things we've been wanting to do for so long."

"I'd always planned to come back one day," he said, in his new deep voice. "We moved several times; then after high school I joined the service where I received my education in computer programming. It was there that I met Missy. I'm starting on a new adventure next month. I'm going to be married. We've shared together so many things about each other's lives, really trying to get to know each other deeply before we take this great step, because we both want it to last — to be a forever life together. When I told Missy about Bear, well — she wanted to meet him. She said she thought Bear had shaped a part of me that was so dear to her. I knew, through all those years, I knew you'd be here and I knew you'd have Bear. Yet, there was just a little apprehension about coming. I thought perhaps one small boy's dream would have slipped from you. You have had so many others year after year. Yet, something deep inside whispered to me that everything would be all right, and that's why I came today."

Words flew quickly as each shared things that had happened during those many years. Bear listened attentively, completely immersed in the sharing of the two. Now, at last, Bear could have a rest. He had experienced a beginning and an ending that became a "from now on" time. He felt warm all over.

The sun was low in the sky as the three emerged from the building. The lights had been turned off, the door had been locked, and three hearts had been healed that day, touched by the miracle of love.

About The Author

Beverley Labrum has been an elementary school teacher for thirty-one years, thirty of which have been with the Murray School District in Murray, Utah. She has written and has published two other books, <u>Willy Whiskers</u> and <u>It's Not My Fault</u>. She has written songs for several musicals written by colleagues which have been performed by Murray school children. In 1993 she received the Utah State Legislature Award in recognition of distinguished service in education, and she was named the Teacher of the Year by the Murray School District for the 1996-97 school year.

About The Artist

John Watson has been drawing and painting with a variety of media for most of his twenty-seven years. A graduate of the University of Utah, he is currently spending most of his time as an interior designer. He and his wife, Melody, live in Sandy, Utah.